S0-BEP-795

SKUNK LANE

SKUNK LANE

Brom Hoban

Harper & Row, Publishers

Skunk Lane

Printed in the United States of America. For information address Harper & Row, Publishers, Inc., 10 East 53rd Street, New York, N.Y. 10022. Published simultaneously in Canada by Fitzhenry & Whiteside Limited, Toronto.
First Edition

Library of Congress Cataloging in Publication Data
Hoban, Brom.
Skunk lane.

Summary: A young skunk named Jarvey Blackpaw leaves home at his parents' bidding, but finds that his music and willingness to work for his room and board serve him well.
[1. Skunks–Fiction. 2. Musicians–Fiction]
I. Title.
PZ7.H6347Sk 1982 [E] 81-47729
ISBN 0-06-022347-2
ISBN 0-06-022348-0 (lib. bdg.)

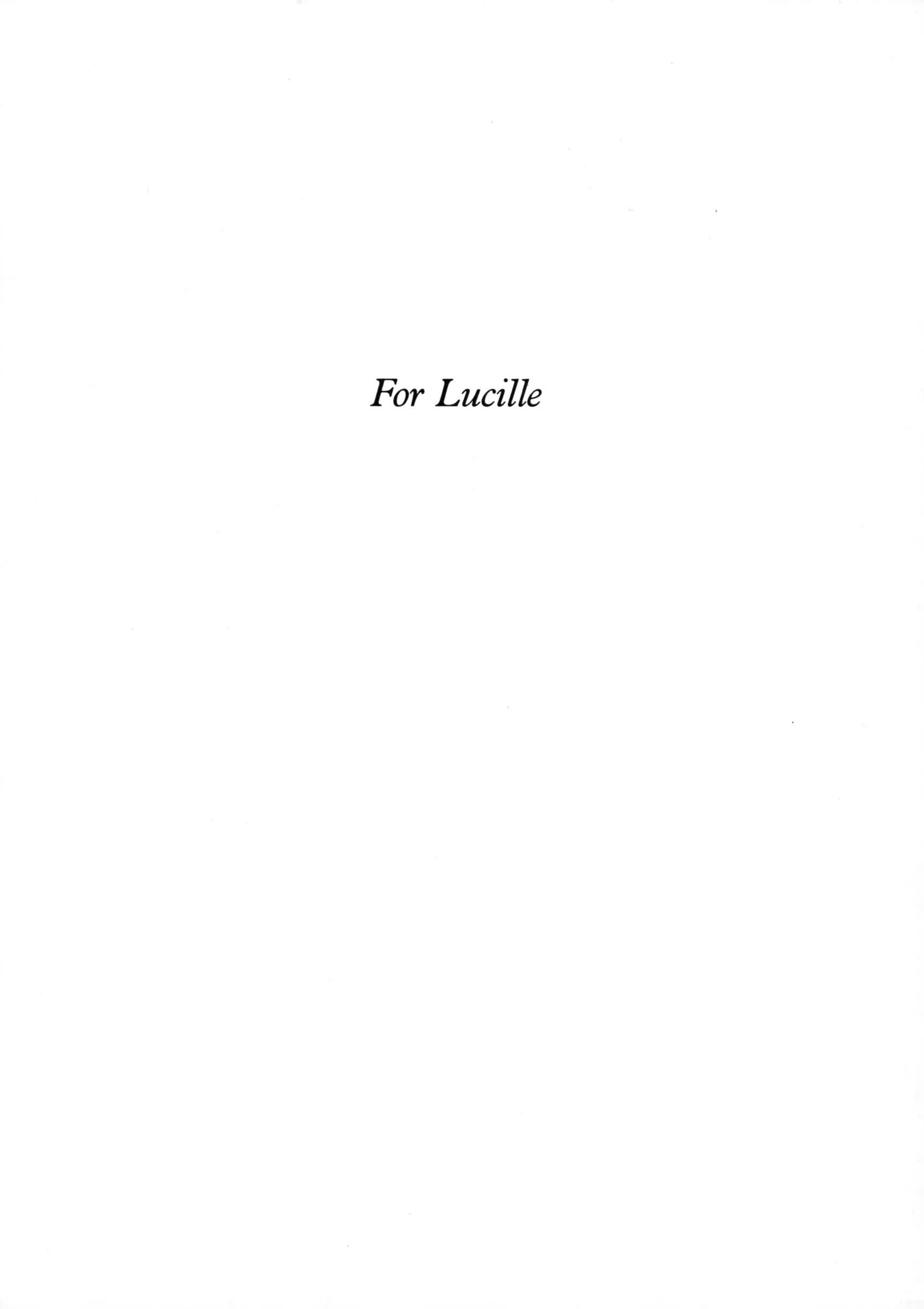

For Lucille

SKUNK LANE

Jarvey Blackpaw was upstairs listening to music. He was listening to his favorite band, The Dirty Rats. Jarvey's room was a mess. There were old socks, orange peels, piles of comics, and many, many other things.

"Jarvey!" yelled his mother. "Come down now! Come down and shuck the corn for dinner."

Jarvey waited until the record was over. Then he went down to help. He had on his old pants, the ones he liked the best. They were too small on him.

"My, how big you have grown," said his father, looking over his paper.

Jarvey smiled and made a muscle.

"Strong, too," he said.

"Strong enough to help out right now," said his mother.

"And big enough to do a lot of other things," said his father.

When they sat down to dinner, Jarvey's father said, "I have been thinking, Jarvey. I remember when I was your age I was a soldier in the first dump war. Nothing but a lot of garbage. Anyway, it made me grow up a lot. I don't think you will ever grow up if you just lie around here."

"I'm doing fine," said Jarvey.

"How about your friend Fred Wetfoot? Isn't he head garbage collector now? He built his own house, too."

"Yes, I know," said Jarvey. "But I don't know what I want to do."

"Well, there is only one way to find out," said his mother. "Your father and I have decided it is time for you to move out."

"You are a big skunk now," said Mr. Blackpaw.

"You mean you are throwing me out?" asked Jarvey with his mouth full.

"You will be glad we did, in the end," said his mother.

Jarvey finished eating without saying anything. Then he went upstairs. He packed all of his things in his knapsack. He packed his sleeping bag, his overalls, and his harmonica. Then he put on his cowboy hat and went downstairs. He took some apples, a bag of walnuts, and some cheese crusts and stuffed them in too.

Mr. and Mrs. Blackpaw were sitting by the fire.

"Bye!" said Jarvey.

"Well, you don't have to leave right now," said his mother.

"You can wait until tomorrow when the sun is out," said his father.

"That's O.K.," said Jarvey. "I know when I'm not wanted." And he went out the door.

"I hope he will be all right," said Mrs. Blackpaw.

"Don't worry, I am sure he will be just fine," answered Mr. Blackpaw.

Jarvey took the old road through the pine forest. It was very dark. He could hear his friends the owls hooting up above. Tonight they did not sound friendly, though.

Once Jarvey saw a large thing ahead of him. He grew a little scared and hid behind a tree. But when the thing passed by, he saw it was only Oliver Possum. "Oliver is probably coming back from a late night out," thought Jarvey. "He is probably coming home to sleep."

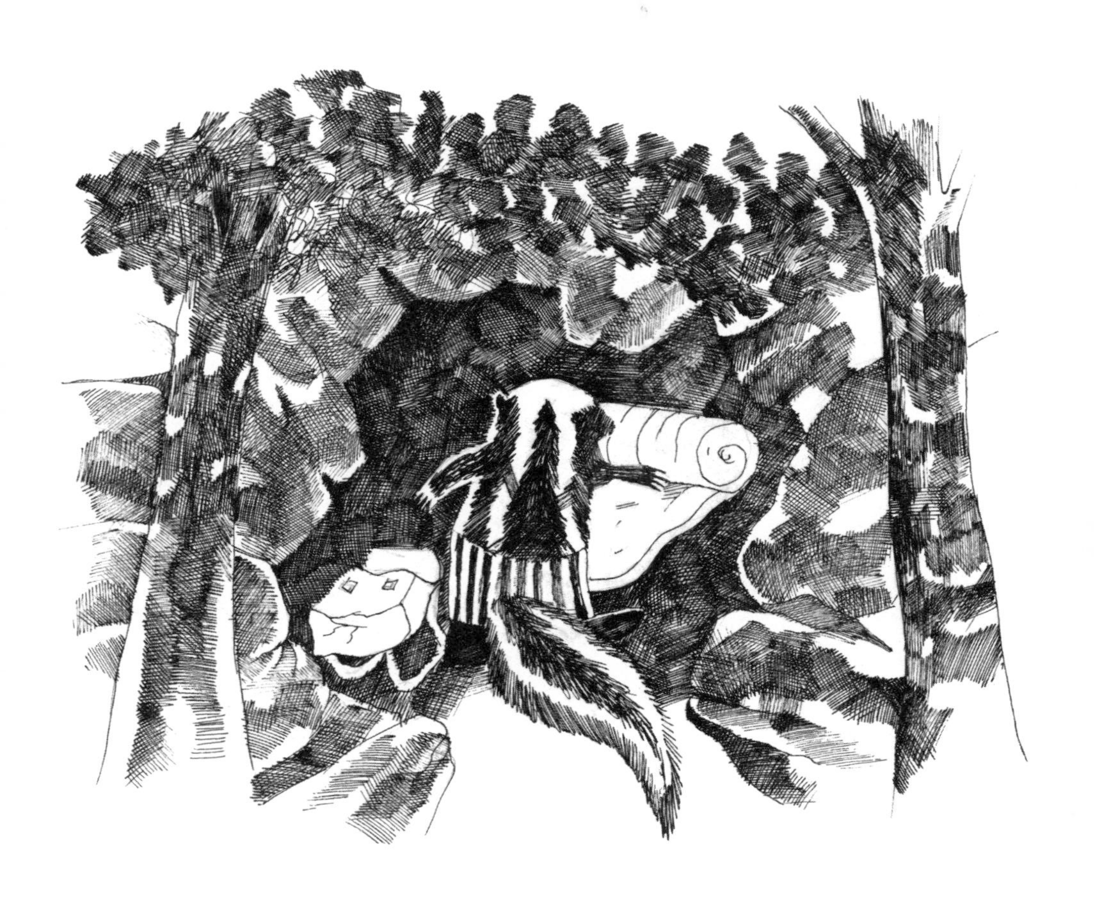

Jarvey walked on a few more miles. After a while he became tired. Jarvey found a small cave and crawled inside. He unrolled his sleeping bag and went to sleep.

Sometime in the night it began to rain. It thundered and there were bolts of lightning, but Jarvey did not wake up.

In the morning Jarvey was all wet. The water had filled up the cave. Jarvey and his sleeping bag were in a pool of water. “This is awful,” thought Jarvey. “I hope things aren’t always this bad.”

Then the sun came out, and Jarvey hung up his sleeping bag to dry. He ate some nuts and played his harmonica. He made up some words to go with the harmonica tune.

Feeling cold and feeling wet—
Things are not much better yet.
With no home you grow up fast;
I hope this feeling does not last!

Jarvey packed up and began walking down the road. Just then he saw someone around the bend. It was Betty-Lou Skunk with her cousin, Mary-Sue.

"Is that Jarvey Blackpaw?" asked Betty-Lou.

"No, I don't think so," said Mary-Sue. "He lives pretty far from here. Must be a tramp."

Jarvey pulled his cowboy hat down low and played his harmonica so the girls would not see his face.

After they went by he felt even worse.

"I have no job and no friends," thought Jarvey. "And if I don't find something soon, I will have no food. Then there will be nothing left to have nothing of."

Jarvey walked all day through the woods.

"At least the sun is shining," he thought when he stopped for lunch. He sat by a little stream and ate an apple and some cheese crusts. Then he saw some blackberries. He ate those too.

"I wonder what I will do now," he thought. He played his harmonica a little bit. It sounded good with the song the river was making. Jarvey sang to the river:

Running gently, running free,
You are not at all like me.
You know where you want to go,
And you'll get there, fast or slow.

When Jarvey stopped singing he could still hear some music. It was coming through the trees. Jarvey started off toward the music. The closer he got, the louder it got. Then Jarvey saw a big green place. There was a sign on it that said "Raccoon's Place." Jarvey walked inside.

He saw a banjo player, a guitar player, and a drummer. There were tables and chairs. It was a place to listen to music.

“Have some tree-frog grog?” someone asked.

Jarvey turned around. It was Raccoon. Raccoon gave Jarvey a big mug of tree-frog grog. “Sit down,” Raccoon said. “Drink some frog grog and have a good time.”

Jarvey sat down. He tried the tree-
frog grog. It tasted funny, but good.

Soon he was tapping his foot to the music. The sun went down over Raccoon's Place. The place began to fill up. Soon everyone was dancing. Jarvey took out his harmonica and started to play along with the band. They were playing "Frog Swamp Stomp."

“Hey! You sound pretty good,” said Raccoon. “Get up there and play with the band, and you can have all the frog grog you want.”

Jarvey got up and began playing with the band. The crowd loved him. They played and played all night and everyone had a wonderful time. Finally there was no one left but the band.

"Well," said Raccoon. "Time to close up. Thank you, and come back."

"I have nowhere to go," Jarvey said to the band. "I'm just a bum."

"Anyone who plays harmonica like that is not a bum," said the banjo player. "You can stay at our place."

"Where do you live?" asked Jarvey.

"Just come with us through the woods," said Fred, the banjo player. "We live on Skunk Lane."

At the end of Skunk Lane was a big, old house. It smelled a little like skunks.

"This is our house," said Fred.

"Everyone who lives here has a job. James finds food. I do all the cleaning. Pierre fixes things."

"How come Pierre has no tail?" asked Jarvey. "What will my job be?"

"He lost it in a fight," said James. "We will find you a job tomorrow."

Fred showed Jarvey his room. It was very dirty. There were cobwebs on the wall, and holes in it.

"Oh well," thought Jarvey. "At least I have a roof over my head."

Then it began to rain. There was a hole in the roof. The hole was right over Jarvey's bed. "Not this again," thought Jarvey, as the first drop hit his face. But he was so tired he just fell asleep.

In the morning the sun was out. It shone through the hole in the roof and woke Jarvey up. He was the first one to get up.

Jarvey walked around his new home. Everything was a mess. But it was not Jarvey's mess.

Jarvey found a hammer and some nails. Then he went upstairs and fixed the hole in the roof. When that was done, he cleaned his room and made his bed. Now he was getting hungry.

"I wonder what there is to eat here," thought Jarvey. He went downstairs to the kitchen. When he opened the cupboard, it was bare. The ice box was bare too.

"Well, I guess I will have to be the one who gets food," thought Jarvey.

He took his knapsack and went out to look for food. He found berries on a bush and nuts on a tree.

Then he found a patch of watermelons.

On the way home he saw an old goat. The old goat gave Jarvey some milk. He put the milk in his canteen. Then Jarvey went home.

Fred, James, and Pierre were still asleep. So he cleaned the kitchen and fixed the table. Then he made a big breakfast. Suddenly everybody was awake.

"Look at all the food," said James.
"The table is fixed," said Pierre.
They all had breakfast together.
"This is wonderful," said James. "I think we should have a party."
"Let's get busy," said Fred. "I will make the invitations."

Fred sent invitations to everyone he could think of. The invitations said:

Come to Skunk Lane for the Big Party
Music and dancing and frog grog - free

Jarvey made a special invitation for his parents. It said:

Parents who are very far
Sometimes forget just who you are.
If you want to see your son,
Then come to Skunk Lane for some fun.

Then Jarvey cleaned up the whole house. He picked fresh flowers and put them in a vase. Pierre made a small stage for the band.

James made good things to eat in the kitchen.

"This will be the best party in the whole woods!" said Jarvey.

Finally evening came. The guests began to arrive. They came from all over. The goat family came, and so did the possums.

The band began to play. Soon there were so many people that Jarvey could not count them.

They played “Skunks on the Run.” Jarvey played his harmonica harder than ever.

Then he stepped down and Raccoon got up and played his fiddle.

They played "Country Coon."

Jarvey danced with Betty-Lou Skunk.

Then Jarvey heard, "We did not know you had gotten so good on your harmonica!"

It was Mr. and Mrs. Blackpaw.

"Well," said Jarvey, "there are a lot of things you didn't know about me."

"We always knew you would grow up to be a fine skunk," said his father.

"We were afraid you were lost somewhere," said his mother.

"I guess you have to be lost before you can be found," said Jarvey.

Then they all joined hands for a family dance.